Minecraft: Final Play

A Minecraft Novel

D1470277

Chapter 1: Click OK to Change Your Reality

It was the strangest convention Rose had ever gone to. There were no bright lights nor booths nor chairs in front of a platform where people were going to speak. When Rosie entered the room where the convention was going to be held, the only thing she saw was a long meeting desk filled with desktop PCs. Each PC was blocked by the other with huge panels, as if each were tiny cubicles filling a single table.

TAKE A SEAT.

That's what all the monitors read. The letters were large and the screen seemed to buzz as the red words pressed into Rosie's eyes. The seats were all numbered from 1-19. Rosie remembered the invitation she received had a number within that range. She took out the envelope and looked at the paper inside again.

Greetings! You have been chosen to attend the greatest Minecraft convention ever! Come on and join us in the Atlantic Building at Marvin Gardens. All attendees will gather at Room 108 at 10 AM. Don't be late! We have a seat specially picked out for you. See you there and have a great time!

She flipped it over and saw the large black number **14**. She scanned the room and found just that number in the middle of the left part of the table. Rosie sat down and immediately the screen opened to the Desktop. The wallpaper was a Creeper breaking out of the Windows screen, something Rosie had overused already on her laptop. As she looked, she found that there was nothing on the Desktop except the oh-so-familiar Minecraft icon, a square Grass Block, at the uppermost corner. She looked at the clock on the computer's taskbar and saw it was five minutes to ten. Where was everyone?

The Minecraft icon seemed to burn into Rosie's retinas. Her fingers hovered over the mouse. I guess there's no harm if I click on it now, is there? Rosie thought. She was sure there wasn't. She opened it and the launcher prompted her to log in.

Username: rosevoid

Password: *************

She clicked log in and the screen loaded. Rosie pressed the Single Player tab and found there were no worlds created yet. Just as she was about to make her own, a dialog box suddenly flashed on the screen.

Please select Multiplayer and The World server.

Rosie obeyed and, as promised, The World was there. She found it a strange name for a world.

Perhaps the convention's committee couldn't think of one. Perhaps they were lazy. Or maybe it had a purpose. It was a simple name, but Rosie could feel the power in the name. The World. She clicked Select. Instead of seeing the words Loading Terrain, something else appeared on the screen of dirt pixels.

Click OK to change your reality.

The OK button was right below this. Change reality? Rosie thought. Is this some kind of joke? It didn't matter, she guessed. She was filled with the strange desire to see The World. She clicked OK and then her vision went dark…

***

Jake found the room the strangest place to have a convention. When he opened the door, he didn't see seats arranged in front of a platform. He didn't see booths, either. Inside the room was a long table with computers lined up and separated from partitions. Each computer had a number ranging 1 to 19.

TAKE A SEAT.

The screens invited him. He had walked some way to get here, having asked directions five times. He was happy to sit at the number written on his invitation. A Minecraft launcher icon appeared on the Desktop. Yes, this was definitely a strange convention. It was especially strange to Jake because it was ten o' clock and almost no one was here. No one was here at all.

Chapter 2: Convention Time

The first thing Rosie saw was water and a square white sun rising high above her. It was something she usually saw just before the world's terrain started loading but what was different was that she could feel. The blue water seemed to surround her completely, her arms moving slowly like sticks in thick syrup. The water was cold and even if Rosie thought she was dreaming, she dared not breathe in fear of choking. Things suddenly became dark and she felt herself hit soft ground.

There was a light breeze in the air and Rosie could feel the warm sun on her skin. Soft grass tickled her legs and arms and face. Rosie opened her eyes and she was amazed by what she saw. Pixels. Small little, lush green pixels just under her face. She stood up and saw a smooth flat surface of green, one so familiar it gave her the creeps. As she scanned the area, she saw everything was in squares, or at least shapes made out of squares. Groups of perfectly straight oak trees and birch. Flat, 2D clouds passed above her where the rectangular white sun was still high in the sky.

It can't be...Rosie muttered to herself. She looked at her hands: white squares with intricate patterns at her risks. She looked at clothes: rose red tunic with bands, long rectangle legs…in the distance she saw pigs—no, rectangle polygons of pigs—roaming around. Rosie felt a chill behind her back but not because she didn't know where she was. Rosie knew exactly where she was.

I'm in the game…Rosie said. Oh, gosh, I'm inside Minecraft!

The sound of chopping grass came from behind her. Rosie whirled around and saw a square green pixilated face, two pixel eyes and a hideous black frown: a Creeper. And with it came the sound just before such a mob exploded.

Sssssst….

***

"Looks like another one's arrived," Olaf said as he stared at the newly spawned player.

The player had the name rosevoid hovering over her head, just as everyone else who had arrived thirty minutes ago did. Olaf's own username awkwardly flashed above him: madpatata83. His avatar was using a custom made skin: a man with black hair, a zigzag scar on one eye and an eye patch on the other. He wore a black tunic and pants, but he was far more impressed by the skin of the new player. The username and the skin suggested she was a girl. She was using the Nether Queen skin, a beautiful cream-skinned girl with pink-red hair and a brown circlet on her. She wasn't too bad made.

Olaf made half the mind to go to her while she was still unconscious, but she woke up soon enough and another user in a Creeper skin was approaching her. Olaf couldn't help but smile. "She won't like seeing him first," Olaf thought. And as expected, he heard a high-pitched scream. It was followed by the quick tick sound you heard when you got damaged inside the game. The new girl was hitting the Creeper-skinned guy with a red poppy item.

"I better go over there…" he said. And he walked along with his arms swinging widely and his legs striding, just as the Minecraft avatar did when it moved in-game.

***

"Aaaaaaaaaaaaaaaah!" Rosie screamed.

She stepped backward while hitting a flower in the process. She picked it up and began charging at the Creeper, causing it to recoil.

"Ow! Quit it!" the voice of a young man squealed. "Do you want to kill me!?"

Rosie looked. The Creeper figure raised its arms in the air, trying to block itself. Wait, arms? Rosie said. Creepers didn't have arms. They were long sticks with a head and four feet. Rosie's hand came to her mouth.

"Oh!" she said in sudden epiphany.

"Oh, what!?" the person—she was sure that's what it was this time—yelled irritated.

Rosie hurriedly walked up to the Creeper-thing, bending over and looking at it in earnest.

"You're a player?" Rosie asked.

The person turned to her, the Creeper face now glaring at her, and a voice came out of it again.

"Of course I am!" he yelled. And then the anger in the Creeper face dropped into a more surprising realization. "Wait a minute...I felt you hit me."

He then looked at himself and jumped, surprised at everything and looking around just as Rosie had a few seconds ago. Rosie got to the conclusion before he could.

"I think we're in-game," Rosie told him quietly. She looked up at his username: theRedman29. The player looked at her.

"This isn't a dream?" he asked. Before Rosie could say yes, he answered himself. "I felt pain. This isn't a dream. It's got to do with that weirdo convention, doesn't it?"

Rosie tried to speak again, but someone else spoke the answer for h.

"Yes it does," a voice said from the distance.

Rosie and theRedman29 looked to their left and saw a player walking towards them. Had the moment not been a serious one, Rosie would have laughed. The name madpatata83 was hanging over this guy's head.

"Who are you?" theRedman29 said pointing an arm at him.

"Can't you see my name?" madpatata83 said too serious to sound like he was joking. "But anyways, don't call me that. My name's Olaf."

"I'm Rosie," Rosie said despite herself.

theRedman29 looked incredulously at the two but then bobbed his head.

"Jake," he replied.

Olaf nodded and then looked at the two.

"I woke up here thirty minutes before you guys," Olaf said. "So that gave me some time to think about this. There are other players here, too, all of which had been invited to the convention. We should go join them in the convention area."

"Convention area?" Rosie was surprised.

Olaf jerked his head backwards.

"This server was made just for us," Olaf said. "You'll see in a few moments."

He began to walk north and for a minute Rosie felt like she was watching a Minecraft movie on a wide panorama screen. But that's not the case, is it? she thought. Jake's Creeper face was no longer mad and when Rosie looked at him he was shrugging, almost saying, Why not? They followed quickly after him, walking on a stair of grass blocks on a hill. From the top of the hill, Jake made a low whistle.

"Now that is sweet!" he said.

Rosie looked in the same direction and instantly held her breath.

At the bottom of the hill was a giant pit crafted into a huge amphitheatre. Quartz blocks were turned into pillars and a semicircular wall. More of them had been used to fill the theatre as seats and stairs. In the middle was a large wooden stage with red wool acting as curtains. Two blocks stood in the center—a podium, Rosie assumed.

Around a dozen more people were down there, already sitting and muttering in worried whispers, wondering what could possibly be going on.

The players only filled up the first two rows, according to number as sign boards were placed on each block. Rosie and Jake found Olaf standing by number thirteen.

"What a coincidence," Jake said lightheartedly. "Looks like we're seatmates."

Rosie nodded, not trusting herself to really talk, but Olaf didn't hesitate to speak at all.

"Assuming we're all from the same convention room," Olaf said. "There should be nineteen people here. Once all the seats are filled up, maybe something will happen."

"You sound like you know a lot," Jake said suspiciously.

Olaf raised his hands in surrender.

"I've been here half an hour before you have," Olaf said. "I've had a lot of time to think."

Jake frowned in Creeper fashion, but said nothing. Rosie sat down in her seat and the two followed. It was then that the stage lighted. Of course, in Minecraft, there were no light bulbs, but there were square lamps powered by Redstone, Minecraft's main energy propellant.

Everyone hushed down. The sky suddenly turned dark, alarming everyone in the process. What if monster mobs come out and get us? Rosie thought. And then she heard the sound. It was indescribable. It was the sound of a screeching whisper. It was the sound of static and wind that made your spine tingle and your eyes go wide agape. It was horrible playing Minecraft and hearing it but now it was even worst. It was the sound of an Enderman.

The Enderman was a three-block high mob black in appearance with bright purple eyes and long limbs. It teleported around the terrain and sometimes picked up blocks. The frightening part was that, if threatened, it gave considerable damage, its mouth wide and gaping like that of a skull, teleporting before you ever got the chance to kill it.

"Rosie?" a voice said.

Rosie jumped in her seat. She was relieved to see that it was just Jake at her right, even if he had the face of a Creeper.

"Did you hear that?" Rosie asked.

"Heard what?"

"The Enderman's sound."

Jake looked at her, puzzled. Rosie listened again, but there was no sound anymore. She shook her head.

"Never mind," she said quietly. "I just don't like it being dark and having no weapon."

Something began blinking on the stage. Rosie and Jake looked as it flickered. A black form, but certainly not an Enderman due to its short height. Staring at it harshly, it was the image of a player in a Grim Reaper skin. Light gray pixels dusted the edges of the pure black cloak. Two red dots for eyes stared at the audience.

Good evening…it said. The voice was loud and husky at the same time. It was a voice that made Rosie want to scream. Everyone looked to where the Grim Reaper was, talking in worry and confusion. The Grim Reaper ignored them.

I'm sure you're all wondering why you're here, it said. The crowd grew quiet. The figure raised its hands in the air like someone of power over the crowd.

I welcome all of you to The World's convention! it said. As you see, all of you are special players, carefully selected to play a game within a game.

"A game within a game," Rosie said aloud, but not questioning it.

It is a game of chance…a game of survival…

Rosie felt a knot twist in her stomach.

It's a game of escape.

The Grim Reaper's red eyes looked at the players, his glare sending the feeling of invisible lasers piercing through their minds. Something seemed to blink above him vaguely and seconds later it was all too hard not to see: large red letters buzzing brightly over his head.

I am REDNE, the man said. I am your game master. Listen to my rules and you just might make it. In The World you will experience Minecraft to the fullest. You will see, hear, smell, taste and feel. You will not only play, but you will fight for your lives because if you don't you die and will never be able to escape The World. You'll be stuck here. Nothing more than a mob for other players to poke at from their computers.

Rosie could hear a girl crying. A guy gasping. Others silent and others who couldn't seem to be grasping it. She looked at Jake whose Creeper face stared blankly at REDNE in denial. Olaf looked like his heart had sunken into his stomach. Rosie felt a drop of sweat trickle down her face and couldn't believe that was even possible.

I will group you all into threes...REDNE said. And from certain points, you must reach the portal at the coordinates I will register for you.

REDNE swayed his hand in the air and a screen appeared in front of everyone. It was the inventory screen. Just like in the game, it showed their avatar in the upper left corner, four crafting boxes on the right and inventory boxes below. In the inventory, there was a Book item.

Go ahead and select it, REDNE said again in the voice that made Rosie want to scream.

Everyone followed and the book showed the rules and coordinates in fine print.

1. Your goal is to reach the portal at (x: 616 z: 358)

2. In groups of three, you will be teleported exactly 7 days of travel from the coordinates

3. Only the first three groups to reach the end will be saved

4. Collect resources and fight as needed

5. You may fight other players, if necessary

6. If you die, you will not respawn as a player, but a mob

7. Enjoy the game.

When Rosie and the others looked up again, REDNE's image began to flicker again. First, subtly, like small blinks, and then they became longer and more obvious until he finally disappeared. Some of the players began screaming. Others sat silently in disbelief. Rosie did this too, closing her eyes, praying this was all a dream. And then it was dark and the only thing Rosie could see was

Loading terrain…

Chapter 3: The World

It's just a dream. It's just a dream. Oh, please, let this be a dream…

But no matter how much Rosie begged, she found herself again on the Grass blocks. Rosie felt like crying, but the panic inside her was so firm it wouldn't lend her the energy to even do that. It was morning again, strangely. She looked around her and almost jumped in surprise. From every side was a steep descent of blocks going down. Stone, grass and dirt toppled over one another, forming a range of hills and mountains. Rosie felt woozy, scared of falling down (she still didn't know what pain might be like in the game) and squatted down.

Why am I here!?

Rosie realized she hadn't said that in her head. Her scream sent a wavering echo throughout the hills.

"Hey!" a voice yelled.

It sounded familiar enough and relief filled her.

"Jake!?' she cried.

"Rosie!" the voice called. "I'm down here with Olaf!"

"Join us!" Olaf said, his strong, deep voice echoing through the hills as well.

"C-coming!" Rosie sent back. She looked down the way she heard the voices coming from. This should be easy, Rosie gulped. Like in Minecraft, you just have to step and step and—

Rosie's foot landed in the air and she began to drop down. She tried to scream, but she couldn't. Her heart seized her and the panic seemed to cut off her voice completely again.

"Oh, my gosh, she's falling!" Olaf's voice came. "Jake, she's falling!"

In Minecraft, drops were only about five seconds, but to Rosie it felt like five minutes. She saw the Grass blocks, the Stone and the Dirt and…there was a large splash sound. Rosie bobbed in one square block of water. She was so surprised she couldn't seem to see Olaf and Jake right in front of her.

"H-huh?" she breathed out.

"Thank Mojang!" Olaf breathed out. He took an arm and slapped it over Jake's Creeper shoulders. "Jake, how did you know she'd land there!?"

"Dang lucky guess," Jake said. He went over to Rosie who was still standing—no, bobbing—in the two block deep water. "You okay?"

Rosie nodded even if she was not okay. She had fallen Mojang-knows-how-many blocks down and she was alive and unhurt.

"You were falling pretty slowly," Jake explained. "I made a water pool to break it."

"Oh," Rosie said in a sharp gasp. "Oh…th-thank you."

Olaf and Jake took her hands and she hopped out of the water. She could feel water dripping from her hair and clothes and, as expected, small pixels of blue were leaving her like droplets.

"That was close," Olaf sighed. "And I guess we're lucky we're all in the same team, too."

"Yeah," Jake said. "No need to call you madpatata83."

TICK!

Jake yelled the minute Olaf punched him in the stomach. Rosie managed to giggle, but Jake was unhappy.

"Dude!" Jake said. "Didn't you hear what that Grim Reaper said? I'll be a mob if I die!"

"You can't die from a light punch," Olaf shrugged.

"REDNE," Rosie suddenly said.

The two looked at her in confusion.

"What?" they asked.

"REDNE," Rosie said. "That was the name of the Grim Reaper who did all this."

Jake nodded in agreement but Olaf pinched his chin with a square hand.

"We can't be too sure, yet," Olaf told them. "He may just be a lackey."

Someone with that powerful glare and insane voice is only a lackey? Rosie thought to herself. I can't just believe that.

"Either way, he's a bad guy," Jake told him.

Olaf nodded and then looked up to the sky. Rosie could see the fine line of his scar as he did. The sun was shining brightly, but it was going down all the same.

"Our priority right now is to get out of these hills and get wood, food and coal," Olaf announced in a leader-like fashion.

Rosie and Jake agreed and they carefully began descending.

"Extreme Hills biome," Jake muttered. "What luck. Hardly any trees."

"We just need to look a little," Rosie reassured. "And we won't have to worry making a house if we dig into the mountain side."

"Where the caves and monsters are?" Jake frowned.

"Not necessarily," Olaf said. "Rosie has a good point. We'll just to dig through pure stone and not the caves. And we can mine from there."

They worked fast and found a group of trees, cut the wood and made a Crafting Table. On a side note, Rosie picked up the Oak Saplings just in case trees would be hard to come by in the future. She just hoped enough Skeletons burned in the sun to drop bones for Bone Meal. Looking at the Book, they had some way to go before they reached the coordinates. The Extreme Hills took most of the day, though, and Rosie's plan of making shelter inside of the mountain took action.

The sun was setting down now and they had managed a 15x15 block room.

"We don't have wool," Jake observed. "We can't make beds."

Olaf shook his head.

"It doesn't matter," he said. "We can't skip the night unless everyone goes to sleep. It's best if we go mining."

Urrgh…

Rosie turned sharply to the door, equipping her Stone Sword. Heart pounding and her head about to explode from fright, she gently edged to the door.

Bang!

Rosie shrieked as the door slightly pushed forward, a mossy green face staring at her from the outside.

"A zombie," Rosie said calmer than she really felt.

"It can't break through the door alone," Olaf said.

Urgh…raarr..urgh…

More sounds came to the door, followed by incessant banging. Rosie could feel the blood dropping to her feet. Zombies had never scared her before. They were the weakest monster mobs to her. They were predictable, easily killed and even gave useless drops. But it was different in The World. Zombies could very well be capable of damaging—killing—Rosie. Rosie looked at Jake and Olaf in a what-do-I-do kind of manner.

"We should mine," Jake said nervously. "Olaf's right after all."

He rushed over to where Rosie stood paralyzed and covered the space of the door with Cobblestone blocks. He dusted his hands.

"That should stop them from getting in even if we break the door," Jake said.

Rosie's face sank.

"I think we're in Hardcore mode," Rosie said. "That concentration of Zombies is only in Hard mode."

Olaf waved a hand in the air and opened his Inventory Screen. He nodded briefly at Rosie.

"It looks like it," he said. "The menu says so right here. The level's locked on Hard."

Urrrgh…raar…urggh!

The groans of the Zombie mobs were followed by a loud crashing sound. The door had broken. Olaf took out his Stone Pickaxe and began digging down. Rosie hurriedly crafted a bunch of torches. She and Jake followed as Olaf mined a single-block wide stair going downwards into the darkness. The narrow walls made Rosie feel breathless in a bad sort of way. She had never been claustrophobic, but the walls of Stone just seemed to be pressing too tight against her. She wondered if they'd run out of breath, but they were breathing just fine by the tenth block. It was usually a long way down in the game, but it didn't take too long for Olaf to stop.

"Whoa," his voice said.

Rosie and Jake tried to peer in front to where he was.

"What is it?" Jake asked.

"Guys…" Olaf said softly. "We've hit a ravine."

***

Somewhere in Midwestern City, a man was at the Atlantic Building, sitting alone in a room full of computers. He watched a multitude of video screens show Minecraft players trying to survive the night. There was an unfortunate group that was in a desert, dodging monster mobs in a desert temple; another group was at sea on boats; and another group was amusingly mining smack dab in the middle of a ravine. The man watched intently as the three clung onto the wall, trying not to fall down to the hard stone ground or the pools of lava nearby.

Now, that's playing Minecraft, the man smiled. He looked up the players' profiles: **13, 14** and **15**.

He read carefully the data he had collected the week earlier. One was good in combat, another in crafting and the girl…that was interesting. She had decided taking expertise in something pretty unique.

The Nether, eh? he said aloud. I wonder how that works exactly. No matter, we'll find out soon enough.

***

Rosie was sweating, but she wasn't that worried about the lava anymore. Thanks to Jake, they were able to make set of stairs going to the bottom from inside the stone walls. They found things in plenty and no monsters seemed to be around…yet.

"It's night time," Olaf explained. "They're all likely outside on the surface."

Rosie nodded. She already knew this, but Olaf's reassurance comforted her. Jake was able to make an Iron Bucket and scooped a block of water from the falls on the edges. He proceeded to flood the lava with water, making the ground hiss and hiss. The floor turned into Obsidian, immediately making everything darker. Rosie planted torches along the path as Jake went ahead merrily flooding the lava, feeling all powerful.

"That's right, keep hissing!" Jake laughed. "Feel the wrath of cool water, Lava!"

"If you fall in, I'd laugh," Olaf remarked.

That joke made Rosie laugh, which felt good. She couldn't imagine being able to do so knowing that her life was on the line. She was actually glad she was with two other people. She could only imagine what it might have been like alone. For example, alone she'd take hours getting enough stuff in order to survive. With all of them here, they had gathered enough Iron to make armor and good tools. They also had a lot of coal. There was one problem, though.

Grumble, grumble.

The three looked to their stomachs. Jake waved his screen.

"We're hungry," Jake said. "Do we still have food?"

Everyone turned to their inventories.

"Just three more Bread," Olaf said. "I say we beat it and head to the top."

Rosie nodded.

"We're also headed in the right direction," she said. "I don't think there's a problem if we just climb up on blocks."

Jake rubbed his chin and nodded as well. They began walking to a wall where they planned to dig up, but Jake stopped abruptly near a flow of lava.

"Diamonds!" he cried.

Rosie and Olaf rushed to where he was looking. The lava was flowing and hovering just above a smaller portion of the cave. Rosie could see the glint of light blue alright, but deep ahead was dark.

"Is it worth it?" Rosie bit her lip.

Jake looked at her as if he thought she were nuts.

"Of course it is!" he yelled. "A long lasting Pickaxe will be handy and it can break Obsidian, which might be needed in the future."

"It's your risk," Olaf said. "Just be careful. We'll be here to douse you if you set yourself on fire."

It was a joke, even in its serious tone, and Jake ignored them. He climbed up on a few blocks and covered the lava with Cobblestone. Slowly, the lava stopped flowing and the lower cave was now open to him. Rosie and Olaf approached cautiously, but Jake was excited. He gave them a smug look.

"You'll thank me for this," Jake said in a sing-along manner.

He continued to walk forward and set up a Torch by the wall. He began mining the Diamonds, counting them merrily as he did.

"One diamond…and a two…and a three…and a…"

Sssssssssst…

Jake whirled around to see a reflection of his avatar…only it wasn't his avatar at all.

"JAKE, LOOK OUT!" Rosie screamed.

A large explosion followed, knocking Olaf and Rosie back to the opposite wall. The Stone crumbled and the lava flowed. Rosie's heart stopped as Jake's bloodcurdling scream filled the air. It was soon enough when his avatar came running towards them in flames.

"PUT ME OUT!" he yelled. "PUT ME OUT!"

Olaf and Rosie ran forward with Water Buckets. Rosie was just about to pour hers until a sharp pain forced her back to the wall. TICK!

"Gah!" she yelled.

She grabbed her shoulder and saw a stick with a feathered end poking out.

Oh, gosh...

Rosie looked up to see a Skeleton in front of her with bow and arrow. Her heart began beating fast and the pain was throbbing in her shoulders but she jumped to the sides all the same just as the next arrow flung into the air. She hit the Obsidian ground hard, her elbows' skin grinding hard on the rough surface. The sting from the cuts was quickly eased though as the water suddenly seeped under her.

"Rosie!" Olaf cried.

A clattering sound was heard as Olaf charged from behind the Skeleton. Rosie saw Jake at the side, recovering from the lava burn. She rushed up again, head dizzy and sidestepped as another arrow flew towards her. She grabbed her Iron Sword and jumped. The gray-white face of the Skeleton connected with the blade and broke down with a rattling sound.

"Ugh…" Jake muttered.

Rosie and Olaf rushed to Jake who was sitting down in the corner. From their peripheral vision, they could see Jake's Health and Hunger. Jake still had half, but his food was low.

"Are you alright?" Rosie said.

Jake looked up dizzily.

"The Creeper…there was a Creeper…"

"We know," Olaf said, but not really out of sympathy. "I told you to be careful!"

"Hey," Rosie said quietly. "There's no time to fight. Jake, eat up and let's head to the surface. I think there are more monsters coming are way."

Olaf's anger simmered down and he nodded.

"She's right," he said. "It's getting close to morning anyway.."

***

By the time they reached the surface, Rosie was exhausted and hungry. The sun was high above their heads and Rosie couldn't help but collapse on the Grass blocks she no longer dreaded seeing. Olaf gave the area a quick scan. They were now in a forest of Oak Trees. Three bright pink Pigs were sniffing around, oinking.

"Food!" Jake cried.

He charged forward and knocked the animals down. Olaf helped Rosie up as Jake set up the Furnace.

"Thanks," Rosie said as she got back up. "Also for earlier."

Olaf shrugged.

"It was something any of us would have done," Olaf said. "And I guess the Diamond can come in handy, though I still think Jake's a complete bozo."

"I heard that," Jake said, though lightheartedly.

Olaf smiled and nodded. At least they're getting along now, Rosie thought to herself. The three sat down on the Grass, enjoying a breeze they would otherwise be unable to appreciate if they weren't in the game. It was something Rosie also couldn't appreciate when she was in the real world, always stuck to the computer and too scared of the outside world.

"It's so peaceful," Rosie said as she ate a Pork Chop in her bare hand. She could actually taste it and it was good, lacked salt, maybe, but good all the same. Jake stretched out his arms and yawned.
"Yeah," Jake said. "I always knew that the Grassland biome was the ideal picnic area."

Olaf sighed in pleasure, too.

"Take it in while you can, guys," he said. "We still have a few days ahead of us."

"A few days…" Rosie muttered. "I wonder just how long that will feel for us."

"Like a few days if you let it," Jake said, biting greedily into his own food. "Who knows? Maybe if we treat it as a game, it will be as easy as a game."

"That's hardly going to be true," Olaf frowned.

Jake shrugged.

"I'd like to believe it if it will get me through everything."

"And I'd like to not trust someone who set himself on fire," Olaf said.

Rosie smiled. She looked to the forest and noticed something strange: a glint of purple.

Suddenly, Jake and Olaf talking was too loud for her ears. There was the buzzing and static…the sound that made Rosie's heart stop. But she also heard fire and the snorting of Pigs. It can't be, Rosie thought.

Rosie got up from her place and began walking towards the woods.

"Rosie?" Olaf asked.

Rosie couldn't hear them. She was in a trancelike state. She walked and walked, letting the sound in her head grow louder and louder and letting the image she saw grow larger and larger. Olaf and Jake followed behind her and they saw it, too.

"A Nether portal…" Olaf muttered. "Why on earth is a Nether portal here!?"

Rosie turned to them with an expression of fascination and dread mixed into one.

"It's for us," Rosie said. "It's gotta be."

Olaf and Jake looked at her in surprise.

"What?" Jake said. "Are you crazy!? Do you have any idea how fast we could get killed in there?"

Rosie shook her head.

"It's not just any place in the Nether," Rosie said. "It's a Nether Fortress…and it's ours."

"Ours?" Olaf said confused.

But Rosie was no longer listening. She was walking fast towards the portal, its swirling purple center enveloping her. Whatever's in here for us should come out good, Rosie said to herself. I should know. I'm the expert.

Loading Terrain…

Chapter 4: The Nether

A new world shimmered in front of Rosie, Jake and Olaf. A world of maroon Nether Bricks and the sound of crackling fire.

"We really shouldn't be here," Jake said. His teeth were chattering but it was obviously not the temperature—which was scorching hot—but the nervousness.

Olaf turned to Rosie suspiciously.

"Rosie, why'd you bring us here?" Olaf asked.

Rosie smiled.

"The Nether's going to act as a shortcut," Rosie said. "I remembered when I first saw the portal."

"What do you mean?"

"Take a few steps while looking at the screen."

The two boys followed while watching their screens. Rosie explained.

"When you travel in the Nether, you're walking a far greater distance than in the Overworld, or the surface," Rosie explained. "The ratio of coordinates of the Nether and the Overworld is eight to one. So walking one block here is eight blocks."

"Wow," Olaf said. "That will save us a lot of time. We might be first if no one else is down here."

"Yeah, that's great," Jake frowned in sarcasm. "Only one problem though: We can die here in five minutes!"

Rosie didn't seem affected by the shout. Instead, she smiled.

"Not really," she said. "Because there's Limbo."

"Limbo?" the boys said in unison.

"How many stacks of Cobblestone or Dirt do we have?" she said without actually answering them.

"Six full stacks," Jake said. "I didn't bother to toss them out. And what in Creepers is Limbo?"

Rosie smiled and pointed upwards. Olaf and Jake looked at her as if she'd lost her sanity.

"The ceiling?" Olaf asked.

"No," Rosie said plainly. "Above the ceiling."

Both were still on the verge of confusion and Rosie couldn't help but burst out: "Oh, come on! You're Minecraft players! Don't you guys know anything about the Nether."

Jake smiled sheepishly.

"Actually," Jake said. "I don't bother that much with the Nether. I like to play in Creative mode.

See, I'm addicted to Redstone mechanisms. I like building."

"I like Survival," Olaf said. "And even if I do go to the Nether here and there, my main priority's the Overworld."

Rosie sighed and looked up the Nether Brick ceiling again.

"The Nether reaches a height of 128 blocks," she said. "But the total of blocks you can build is 256. Above the Nether's ceiling of Bedrock is a space without monsters or things. It's just Bedrock and empty space. We can travel there to the Coordinates and just make a portal to the Overworld."

"And the Bedrock?" Jake asked desperately.

The smile on Rosie's lips returned.

"Oh, I know how to get past that alright," Rosie said. "…but we need boats."

"Boats?" the two asked in unison.

Just before Rosie could answer, she heard a sound. It was a high-pitched whispering sound. There were other sounds, too. The husky roar of the fiery Blazes. The oinking of Zombie Pigmen…

"We should get moving," Rosie said. "But first we have to take down this portal's Obsidian."

Jake's Diamond Pickaxe did come in handy after all. After a few anxious minutes, the portal had been torn down.

"You say we just have to go up again?" Olaf asked.

Rosie nodded.
"But I'd rather we find an empty space with a high ceiling to do it," she answered. "I don't want to risk lava."

"The way Jake did?" Olaf smiled smartly.

TICK!

Olaf groaned as Jake hit him with an Iron Sword. He glared at Jake.

"Now, that was out of line!" Olaf shouted. "That's a sword."

Jake just smiled with his Creeper face and twirled the sword.

Haaarr…

A sound came from one of the pathways behind them. Rosie tugged on the boys.

"Keep quiet and let's go," she said. "That's a Blaze. Or maybe they're Blazes."

They rushed towards the long stretch of Nether Brick and eventually saw an open bridge leading to the main part of the fortress. Like most Nether fortresses, they were usually just rectangular blocks, but the sight of seeing a Nether fortress up close took Rosie's breath away. The Netherrack ceiling soared above them in the shape of an uneven dome. Bright falls of lava oozed downwards into spills of gold and red. Zombie Pigmen, humanoid versions of Minecraft pigs with decaying parts, were ahead watching from both sides of the bridge like guards.

"Don't hurt them," Rosie told Jake and Olaf. "They won't hurt us if we don't hurt them. They're neutral mobs. Don't even hit them by accident."

"I know that," Olaf said. "We'll just pass by them."

Rosie scanned the sky for Ghasts, but they were out of hearing for now. She heard something like sloshing inside puddles. She looked down from the bridge to see Magma Cubes hopping—no, plodding— beneath them.

"Do you see any Blazes?" Rosie asked them.

Olaf went past the Zombie Pigmen and peered at the corridor ahead of them.

"We're clear," Olaf said.

"Even from behind," Jake added.

Rosie nodded and they marched ahead, Rosie equipped with a bow while the two boys held their swords. They had to make a turn and eventually reached a small well of lava which Jake scooped up with a bucket.

"It might be useful," Jake said. "I can make something with us."

Rosie smiled.

"I'll trust you on that."

They made a turn and found a stairwell leading up, Nether Warts growing in beds at the side like oddly shaped red mushrooms. Rosie picked them up along with the Soul Sand they were planted it.

"I can make Potions," Rosie said, almost announcing. "But we'd need the drops of other Nether mobs."

"Can we risk that?" Olaf asked her.

Rosie frowned.

"I guess not," Rosie said. "But if ever we do have to fight a mobs here and they leave drops, it can be handy in combat."

They didn't have to, though. They reached the rooftop of the Nether Fortress after climbing the stairs. They had passed a Chest on the way and found Gold Horse Armor and Ingots.

"I'd like to ride a Horse now," Jake had said. "Hi-ho, Silver! Away!"

"But that's Gold Horse Armor," Rosie had pointed.

Jake had shrugged at this.

At the rooftop, Rosie again scanned for Ghasts, somewhat uneasy about making the climb up and a Ghast appearing form nowhere, but again there were none. It's almost scary there's none, Rosie said. I thought we were on Hard mode.

She decided not to complain and the group started up on three pillars of Cobblestone. The climb was an anxious one, scared of falling down any minute to the lava pools below or having a Ghast shoot them off their pillars., but finally Olaf shouted: "I hit Bedrock!"

Rosie and Jake dug into the ceiling of Netherrack as well and found it.

"Okay," Rosie shouted as they were all a few blocks apart. "You have the Boats I crafted earlier, right?"

Both nodded.

"Just do what I do," she said.

She dug one block down so there would be more space between her and the ceiling. She then placed a block in front of her and put the Boat there, one block of air between it and the ceiling. She then placed another Boat lodged on the thick ceiling due to the space between it and the second Boat. She looked at Olaf and Jake and were glad to see they had done exactly the same.

"Access the Boat in the ceiling," Rosie said. "It will bring us there."

"Alright!" the two yelled.

"On three!" Rosie shouted.
"One…two…THREE!"

The scenery blinked before them and then everything was dark for a split second. The next second it was still dark, but in a shadowy kind of way. She placed a Torch in front of her and could see Olaf and Jake. Jake whooped in joy.

"Whoa, we actually made it!" he cried out in joy. He took Rosie by the shoulders and shook her. "Rosie, you're a genius!"

Rosie smiled shyly. Olaf shook his head in disbelief, but gladness that it had worked out.

"Alright," Rosie said. "We'll just have to walk it from here and reach the coordinates."

The two agreed and they began walking, looking the coordinates as the numbers increased and decreased and moved closer to the numbers they had in mind. It was a pretty long walk, but they didn't need to worry much about hunger because there were no mobs up here.

"A day's walk would be eight day's walk here, right?" Jake asked Rosie.

"Yep," she said. "So, we don't have to walk so much, but just have to skip along."

"So, how did you know about this, Rosie?" Olaf then asked in curiosity.

Rosie gave a sly smile and happily replied.

"My brothers introduced me to Minecraft only a year ago and I was immediately hooked," Rosie said. "I spent day after day in the Overworld but it eventually got boring. I then saw my brothers playing using potions, so I asked where they got the ingredients."

"And they told you they came mostly from the Nether," Olaf said.

"Yeah," Rosie agreed. "I made a portal myself so I could hunt for them. And I didn't just spawn in the Nether, either."

"You spawned in a fortress?" Jake said.

Rosie nodded.

"All the loot in the Nether Fortress drove me mad," she said. "I loved the satisfaction of picking of Blaze Rods and Nether Wart. I enjoyed making potions and I've memorized all the formulas. It gives you an all powerful feeling, ruling a Nether Fortress. That's why I'm using the Nether Queen skin."

Jake gave a low whistle.
"Well, you're…um…intense," he said.

Rosie giggled.

"I guess you could put it that way," she smiled.

Olaf seemed to agree with the remark and smiled, too. He was planting more Torches in the way as he watched the coordinates on the invisible screen. He stopped as he placed a sixth Torch on the floor.

"Rosie?" he said.

"Yes?" Rosie said a little bit too cheerily.

"Do things spawn here naturally?"

"No," Rosie shook her head.

"There's something out there."

"What?" she asked. She looked further to a moving figure and was shocked, but not because it was a mob.

"It's a player!" she said.

"What!?" the boys asked in unison.

The group ran closer and saw a player with brown hair, a blue shirt and pants: the basic Steve skin.

"Hey!" Rosie called. "Hey! Do you need help!?"

The Steve-skinned player turned to them, but didn't move closer. He began planting Soul Sand in three columns.

"What's he doing?" Olaf asked.

Rosie looked as the three blocks of Soul Sand were placed in a height of three blocks. Rosie didn't understand it. Was he trying to tell them something? Was he messing with them? Rosie looked closer and then saw something in his hand that made all of Rosie's blood leave her face.

"He has Wither Skulls," she said. "Oh my gosh, he has Wither Skulls…"

"What, Rosie?" Jake said. "What's he doing there?"

The Steve player placed a head on each column of Soul Sand and Rosie finally understood. A blue, three-headed monster appeared. Rosie grabbed Jake and Olaf.

"RUN!" she yelled.

Aaaaaaaoooorrr…

There was a huge explosion.

The Beginning?

Chapter 5: The Wither

A strong, dull pain filled Rosie's body and her head was spinning heavily. She could see Jake and Olaf at her sides, sprawled on the floor and groaning. She tried to remember what happened and at the moment of recall, she leapt from her space to the two. Olaf was getting up but Jake was knocked out cold.

"Get up!" she cried. "Get up! There's a Wither!"

"A what!?" Olaf said as he staggered standing up.

"A WITHER!" Rosie screamed.

Olaf's eyes widened.

"What!?"

"Just help me lift Jake and RUN!" she yelled.

Aaooooorrrrrr….!

The sound came from behind them. Rosie looked, paralyzed as she stared up to the monster. It stood tall above with three black heads and white eyes on each. It's body was nothing but a black rib cage and spine. The moment it locked eyes on them it screeched, shooting three blue Wither Skulls at them.

"DUCK!" Rosie cried.

They ducked down, the Wither Skulls shooting beyond them and exploding on impact. The Wither cried again as Rosie and Olaf stumbled away carrying Jake. Rosie began slapping Jake's cheeks.
"Jake, wake up!" she cried. "Wake up, DANG IT!"

Tick!

She had punched him. Jake recoiled a bit back but his eyes opened.

"Oww…." Jake said.

Rosie gasped, worried she had lowered his Health to a lethal level. She looked at his bar but all the hearts were black. The Wither's hit turns all hearts black…Rosie thought. It's impossible to tell how much health we have.

"I'll distract it!" Olaf called. "Get Jake away and make the portal!"

"No!" Rosie said. "Olaf, don't do it!"

But Olaf had hit the Wither with an arrow. It screeched again, making each part of Rosie cringe to life. She had to focus. She knelt down beside Jake.

"Jake!" she said as she shook him up. Jake looked at her dazed.

"Rosie…?" he slurred.

"Jake, snap out of it!" she yelled. "Help me make the portal!"

Jake shook his head and looked at her, his eyes more focused now.

"A what?"

"A PORTAL, DANG II!"

Jake looked surprised but another explosion sounded in the air. Jake turned to see Olaf running in circles as the Wither monster chased him.

"What in Mojang's name is—"

"It doesn't matter!" Rosie screamed. "Just help me build the portal and let's get out of here!"

Jake stood up and handed her some Obsidian. They quickly started. Hang on, Olaf, Rosie said. We're almost done. Just don't die!

Olaf was a good twenty five blocks away from them, the Wither hovering and shooting aimlessly, but not reaching Rosie and Jake.

"That's right! Come after me!" he yelled as he shot more arrows.

The creature shouted and recoiled, but continued to fire. The ground seemed to shake under Olaf's feet and he could hardly sprint anymore. But it was better he was doing this than the other two. I'm the combat guy, he said. I always have been. Building's just not my thing. The arrows were doing close to no damage. The Wither regenerates…he thought. I can't beat this thing. I just have to stall.

As he turned around a black skull charged towards him. It connected and a loud burst was heard.

"Olaf!" Rosie cried out.

The pain was like hitting a concrete wall. Olaf groaned, the hazy black void of the Nether almost a complete blur. He shook his head, heavy with pain, and tried to focus. His hearts were black and he could hardly believe he was still alive.

"OLAF! WE'RE DONE!" Rosie screamed.

Olaf looked and saw the swirling purple of the portal. He ran towards it as the Wither ran after him. He turned and the Wither was shooting more skulls. Olaf sprinted, zigzagging as he did, barely dodging the skulls as they crashed on the ground, hot and painful. Rosie and Jake were up ahead, Jake waving his Diamond Pickaxe in the air, Rosie jumping like a madwoman. They were five blocks away…four…three…two…

"GET IN!" he cried.

The three were absorbed into the purple and the image seemed to haze before them.

Aaaaaaoooooooorrrrr…..!

The Wither cried. But the monster was no longer in vision.

***

"At least they weren't stupid enough to try and kill it," a hollow voice said in the empty computer room. He sipped his coffee and watched as the three frantically tore down the Nether Portal and then collapsed onto the floor. He looked at their coordinates. They were only a day away from it now.

"I was sure they'd die by the Wither," the voice sighed. "But never mind. I'm beginning to like how they work …"

He left their screen and watched as another group of players on horses was coming the group's way.

"Company?" he asked. "This should be good. Or maybe, bad, if someone causes a little uproar…"

Loading Terrain…

Chapter 6: PK

It was almost an hour before any of them spoke. After destroying the Nether Portal, the three collapsed to the floor, panting heavily and looking at their Health bars which each held only one heart. They weren't regenerating either because their Hunger had dropped again. It was only until their breathing had settled and they were staring blankly at the sky that Jake said something.

"We almost died," he said with no hint of emotion.

Rosie closed her eyes and placed a hand to her forehead.

"I'm so sorry…" Rosie said. "It's all my fault. I should've never led you guys to the portal."

"Don't be stupid," Olaf argued as he sat up. "It's not like you were the one who built that Wither."

Rosie and Jake also sat up, Rosie slouching over in shame despite what Olaf said.

"Still," she said. "We could have just gone on here in the Overworld. I was stubborn."

"Hey, quit blaming yourself," Jake said in a joking manner. "What matters is we're here and only a day away from our destination."

He then stopped smiling and looked at his two teammates apologetically.

"I'm sorry I didn't really help," Jake said. "I probably caused us a lot of time being blegh and stuff."

Rosie shook her head.

"I think you took the most damage from the explosion," she said. "It's amazing I even got to wake you up."

She then turned to Olaf.

"And none of us would've gotten out if you hadn't stalled for us. You could've died doing that."

Olaf shrugged.

"You guys would have done the same if I was unconscious."

They sat there for a few more minutes before getting up. They were in the Desert now and Rosie could still feel grains of sand sticking to her from their lying down. It was fortunate that Jake had killed Pigs in plenty during their last time in the Overworld.

"We have a day's walk," Olaf said.

"A day," Rosie repeated slowly. She savored the last word, letting it roll off her tongue like a piece of meat. "We just need to hang in there a little more and…"

"And it's over," Jake finished.

The words eased Rosie a little, the aftershock of encountering a Wither now dwindled down to a fast heart beat.

"There is one problem, though," Jake said. And they all knew the answer to that.

"That player who made the Wither," Rosie answered. "And it's strange, too, because I didn't see a name over his head."

"He could very well be REDNE," Olaf mused. "Trying to sabotage the groups."

I will group you all into threes…Rosie remembered. And then she halted.

"Wait a minute," she said.

Her teammates stopped as well.

"What is it?" Olaf asked.

"He said he'd group us into threes," Rosie said. "We're nineteen players. Nineteen isn't divisible by three. Someone's left out…or rather…"

"Someone's not really part of this game at all," Olaf said.

Rosie looked at them worriedly.

"Do you think REDNE's disguised as a player?" she said.

"That or he has a bogey," Jake said. "But at least we know it's none of us."

They stood there for a little, quiet. He can come back and attack, all the same, Rosie thought.

"Well," Jake said breaking the silence. "He's not going to be part of a group, that's for sure. If he's the odd one out, he's bound to be alone."

"Not really," Olaf said. "If this bogey is REDNE or is with him, he could easily take a player out and replace him."

"He'd kill his own players?" Rosie asked. "I'm not sure…If I wanted to kill someone that way, I wouldn't have settled for a game like this. I'd want them to die at the hands of the Minecraft world."

Olaf shrugged.

"Either way, we should be careful," Olaf said.

They marched on ahead, the day stretching out fast like warm taffy. There weren't any woods or mountains in the area. It was still bright but dusk was just a couple of hours away.

"And we're out of Cobblestone," Olaf added. "We'll have to seek shelter down under."

"And get buried alive in sand?" Jake said. "I have a better idea. I'll make Cobblestone."

Rosie looked at him surprisingly.

"Make Cobblestone?" she asked.

"He means a Cobblestone generator," Olaf said.

"Yeah," Jake said. "We'll have enough by sundown to make a small hut for the night. And if time doesn't go too fast, maybe a small house."

He set to work immediately by making Pistons which were wooden panels that would push blocks. He then made walls from Sand and Dirt blocks, letting water flow from one end and lava at another. They formed a single Cobblestone block at the center.

"Just one?" Rosie asked.

"Of course not!" Jake said enthusiastically. "I'm going to set up Pistons and Redstone charges."

Jake explained as he did just that on the floor.

"The Piston's going to automatically push the Cobblestone forward with the Redstone powering it," he explained. "Every time the Piston pushes a block out, the lava and water will mix again to make a new one. It gives you an unlimited supply."

Rosie smiled and then laughed sheepishly.

"I could never figure out how Redstone worked," Rosie said. "And remembering the recipes for Redstone stuff bores me, unlike those for potions."

This made Jake smile proudly and he set down the last thing he needed: a Lever. He looked at it as he dusted his hands.

"Looks like it's ready to run," he said. Rosie nodded in consent and he turned it on.

The Piston roared to life, creaking as it pushed the Cobblestone forward into a long strip. The Redstone charges and torches hissed. The loud sound and movement made Rosie laugh out in surprise.

"It's working!" she cried.

"Of course it is," Jake said with a hint of arrogance. "And trust me, this is one of the easier mechanisms out there. I'm able to make draw bridges, elevators…"

"Players up ahead!" Olaf called.

Rosie and Jake turned, not sure of what they heard.

"What?" Rosie asked.

Olaf pointed ahead, moving images coming from the West on Horses.

"Players!" Olaf said. "It looks like a group's caught up with us."

Rosie cupped her hands for a better look and, indeed, there were three horse-riding players coming their way. They all wore Iron Armor and their Horses were clad in armor, too.

"Ahoy there, players!" the voice of a cheery girl cried from the distance. "Have any room for us tonight!?"

Rosie could hear her thoughts repeat. Groups of three…someone's left out, or rather…

***

The players that had shown up were from the numbers **10** to **12**. Number **10** was a girl named Elli, a custom-skinned player with a high yellow ponytail and a rainbow sweater. Number **11** was named Tim, a person with the skin of an old wizard, which reminded Rosie of the one in The Sorcerer's Apprentice. Number **12** was another guy named Luke, who wore black hair and olive skin. He spoke arrogantly and didn't seem to care much for Rosie and her teammates.

"We could've just kept riding," he had complained when everyone sat in the square house they had built later on. They were eating and sitting by the Furnace. "Elli, we could've kept riding all the way and been first. Now we have to tie up with these guys."

"Hey," Jake warned. "It's easy enough to kick you out and leave you in the dessssssert."

He emphasized on the s sound the way Creepers hissed. Elli looked at the group apologetically.

"Don't mind him," Elli said. "He's just stressed. We've been riding almost four days straight and we need a rest. See, we haven't bothered gathering enough to build shelters."

"Did you say four days?" Rosie said surprised.

Elli looked at her confused.

"Uh, yeah," Elli said. "That's how long it's been."

Rosie, Olaf and Jake looked at one another, all thinking about the Nether. It must have sped up the time, too, Rosie thought. She then smiled at Elli and shook her head.

"Yeah, I forgot," she answered. "I haven't really been counting the days."

"Who does?" Tim said. "It makes this Hades even harder."

Elli nodded in agreement while Luke rolled his eyes. Luke then turned to Olaf and squinted.

"Say," he snorted. "How come you're here so fast? I don't see you with Horses."

Rosie didn't know how to answer but Olaf did.

"We used Boats," Olaf said.

It was true, after all, though they didn't use it in the sense that they crossed a sea. It seemed to appease Luke's suspicions and they all sat there for a while. They ended up discussing the convention and everyone had the same back story: they were invited and they opened the Minecraft icon then teleported to The World.

"I wonder how this is even scientifically possible," Elli said.

"I just want out," Jake muttered.

It was dark now, but they weren't worried about mobs. The group had built an Iron Door and as long as they didn't look outside, they'd be fine for the night.

"I think we should all go to sleep," Elli suggested. "I'm exhausted."

Jake yawned and stretched back in his own corner.

"That sounds like a good idea," he said. "We can take turns watching just in case something bad happens."

"I'll take watch," Olaf volunteered.

"What?" Rosie said. "Of course not. You took the most beatings earlier from the…err…mobs."

Olaf looked at her in appreciation, but shook his head.

"I'm fine," Olaf said. "I can't really sleep yet anyways. And night will only last a bit."

Rosie didn't seem happy with his answer.

"I'm okay, Rosie," he said. "All of you get some shut eye."

Rosie found it hard to think of sleeping, but she drifted off easy enough. The Furnace stopped crackling and even the monsters outside didn't seem to bother her as she slept on the sandy floor. She didn't expect to dream, either, but she did. In her dream, she was nothing but floating eyes, looking at an dark sky and pale yellow stones with craters…End Stone. Thick pillars of Obsidian soared to the sky and the insane sound of static and whispered screeches again filled her ears. She watched as long, slender giants with purple eyes went around in what she knew was their domain. The Endermen carried block after block and planted them, each block turning and fusing into End Stone. And then there was a roar in the sky. The Endermen gathered to the center and began to look to the sky. The sound of large, batting wings and blowing wind came to Rosie's ears but when she looked up she saw nothing but darkness.

***

"Rosie!" Jake's muffled voice yelled.

Rosie woke to being shaken up, a warm pink twilight pouring in from the small holes of the Iron Door.

"Uh….?" Rosie slurred as Jake came into her vision.

"Rosie!" he said. "Olaf's gone missing!"

***

"Luke and Olaf are gone," Elli said nervously. "I didn't even notice them leave. I just woke up and they weren't here.

A feeling of worry rushed over Rosie. Where could they have possibly gone? Rosie couldn't imagine Olaf and Luke leaving without even telling anyone. REDNE could have easily taken the place of a player...the words echoed in Rosie's head. Rosie smashed the voice before she could try to comprehend it.

"What's important is that we try to find them," Rosie said quietly. "I'm sure they couldn't have gone that far."

"Should we split up?" Tim asked, one of the few words he'd said the whole time.

Jake frowned at the idea.

"So we'd go missing, too?" Jake said. "I say we go in one direction and come back here in an hour just in case they come back."

Rosie looked as the desert stretched out into the horizon. Please be okay, Olaf, she heard herself wishing. They started walking while Elli and Tim rode their horses on ahead. They called for Luke and Olaf by name, but had no luck. The sun was beating down hard on them and making Rosie feel less worried and more irritated. It was a good thing they weren't that Minecraft had no

Thirst feature or she'd be way over the wall before they reached the end of Desert.

"Hey, guys!" Elli called. She rode back towards them.

"What is it?" Jake asked.

Elli pointed forward.

"There's a small structure over there," she said.

Rosie and Jake rushed after Elli as her Horse galloped to a small Sandstone pyramid. There was no door, but the inside was dark enough. But another thing that caught their eye was Luke's Horse tied down to a fence next to it.

"Do you think they're in there?" Tim asked as his Horse drew nearer to them.

"It's worth checking," Rosie said. "Though it looks dangerous."

"We'll all go," Elli said. "You and Jake go on ahead to see if there are traps. We'll just tie up our Horses."

Rosie and Jake went stepped forward to the small entrance. Rosie put a torch up. It was a small square space with a Sand floor and Sandstone walls.

"There's nothing here, guys," Rosie said. "It's empty."

But as she turned Jake fell over her and they landed on the ground. It wasn't a hard hit, but Rosie was surprised as the Torch came away and something began hissing.

"It's a trap!" Jake yelled.

BOOM!

The loud explosion tossed Rosie and Jake against the wall and the Sand sank down. Rosie tried to grasp onto something, but there was nothing but blank walls. She screamed as she and Jake tumbled down into the darkness, sharp things pricking her at the sides, her Health going down by half a hear each second.

"Rosie, they're Cacti!" Jake said. "Stay still!"

Rosie obeyed and she tried to see in the dark. A faint light came from above and she could see Elli's head.

"Elli, stop!" Rosie cried. "Don't fall down, there's Cacti here!"

But Elli didn't have the face of shock on her. Instead, she smiled.

"Oh, I knew that," she said. "If I didn't, I wouldn't have led you here!"

Rosie's eyes widened and her mouth dropped. Elli laughed.

"What?" she giggled. "Did you really think we needed shelter for the night? That's stupid. And don't think we didn't see you break down a Nether Portal."

Jake growled in anger and raised a fist to the air.

"You creeps!" he yelled. "Don't you know what happens if we die!?"

Elli hummed and tilted her head.

"I do," Elli said. "But you won't die…not yet, anyways. We just want to make sure we're first, that's all."

Elli's head disappeared for a while and another figure came into view.

"Olaf!" Rosie cried.

Before Olaf could look down, he was pushed and he fell in between the Cacti as well, grunting as he hit the floor.

"Olaf, you're alive!" Jake said.

Olaf glared at Elli's face above.

"Yeah," he said. "Luke pretended to storm out and I followed him. He held me up and took everything in my inventory…"

"So noble of you," Elli said. "Your stuff will come in handy. But we're not finished. Rosie and Jake have to toss up everything, too, or I'll blow up the TNT under your feet."

That made Rosie jump and she looked below. She could make out the small pixels of dynamite sticks.

"Why would you do this?" Rosie said. "We're all victims here, aren't we!?"

Elli didn't break into sympathy. She looked at Rosie coldly.

"This is a survival game," Elli said. "And a race. I want to make sure I get out alive."

Rosie couldn't say anything. Her voice had left her. She was angry and in shock at the same time.

"Give everything you have now!" Elli demanded. "I know what you guys have, too. I viewed it last night."

"How did you…"

"I'm a hacker," Elli said. "I know things. Now toss it up!"

Rosie and Jake reluctantly gave threw up their stuff one by one, not even blocks left with them to be able to climb out. Elli smiled cruelly.

"Hope you like your new home, guys," she said with a wave. With that, she blocked the door with two Obsidian blocks. There was complete darkness again. They could hear the voices outside. They could hear the hooves of the Horses treading on the sand.

Did you get everything? A voice asked. It was Luke.

Yeah, Elli said. They fell for the bait.

We'll get to the end in no time, Tim added. They have it all: ores, food, blocks…

Luke's voice was low and gave out a quiet laugh.

Good. He said. I want you guys to have something.

What is it? Elli asked greedily. Wait. What is that? Flint and steel? Why on earth would we want that?

TICK! TICK! TICK!

Luke! What are you doing!? Are you trying to burn us—aaaaaaaaaaaaah! Fire! Put me out! Put me out! Tim!

But Tim began screaming, too. The ticking of their damage seemed to last for seconds.

Stop it, Luke! Elli begged. I thought we were a team! STOP!

TICK! TICK! TICK!

The fire crackled loudly and Rosie, Jake and Olaf stood silently as they listened in horror. The screams stopped and so did the fire crackling. It was followed by a plop, plop, plop! It was the sound of someone picking up a drop.

"He's a PK…" Jake said in a whispered voice.

"A w-what?" Rosie stuttered. She looked at Olaf questioningly.

"PK," Olaf repeated. "He's a Player Killer."

Loading Terrain…

Chapter 7: Last Day's Travel

The last thing Rosie needed to do was cry. It was no help, crying. It would just make her face cringe, make it hard to breathe and embarrass her in front of Jake and Olaf. But cry she did. It came suddenly, too. The moment she heard the words Player Killer, her voice tore open into a sob and she was crying.

"Why!?" Rosie yelled. "Why would someone do that, here!?"

"Rosie…" Olaf said softly.

"No!" she said. "Why are people so messed up!? Why would they set up this game!? Risk people's lives! I don't get it!"

"Because people are screwed up, Rosie," Jake said in a low voice. "But it doesn't mean we are. We can still break out of here. We can finish the game and who knows? Maybe we can save Elli and Tim from being mobs forever. Please don't cry, Rosie. We need to keep it together if we're going to finish this as a team."

Rosie looked up, her eyes feeling swollen and red though her avatar wasn't going to show it.

"Team," Rosie said with a choked voice. "Yeah, we have to…have to…I'm sorry."

She coughed the last of her sobbing and wiped her eyes. She breathed in and out deeply. When she thought she could manage looking at her teammates, she turned to them.

"Sorry," she said. "I was overwhelmed there for a minute."

"It's okay," Olaf said.

She nodded.

"We need to get out," Rosie said. "But how? We're caved in and we don't have tools."

"I do," Jake said.

Rosie looked at her surprised.

"Huh? How? Elli should have known if you kept it from her."

Jake rolled his eyes.

"She was bluffing," Jake said. "I know hackers. They don't announce they're just that. And her eyes were looking to the left. In fact, she's pretty dumb. I had Obsidian but she didn't wonder where the Diamond Pickaxe was. Anyways, I have Cobblestone, a Diamond Pickaxe and Pork Chops…still warm."

If it weren't for the Cacti poking out on every side of Rosie, she would have leapt towards Jake in a hug.

"I have stuff, too," Olaf said. "No matter how bad Luke beat me up with his Sword."

Rosie smiled and then lowered her head.

"I'm so gullible," she said. "I gave everything."

Jake waved his hand lightly, careful not to touch the spiky cactus on his right.

"Don't sweat it," he said."Let's climb up and be on our way."

Jake and Olaf hacked away the Cacti, making Rosie relieved to be able to stretch out again. She looked up to the small ceiling and Olaf handed her some Iron, Cobblestone and Torches.

"We'll craft you armor later," Olaf said and then also jumped up.

They didn't break the Obsidian, but broke out through the softer Sandstone. The sun was still bright on their faces. The Horses of Elli, Tim and, strangely, Luke were there just wandering in the middle of the desert.

"Why would Luke leave his Horse?" Rosie asked aloud.

"Maybe he didn't need it," Olaf said.

Jake shuddered.

"You're not saying he's the bogey, is he?" Jake asked.

Olaf shrugged.

"Anything's possible. But for now, let's get riding. The day's still young and the Horses will make our way to the end."

Each of them took the Horses and sat down on the saddles. Rosie was shaking. She had never ridden a Horse in real life and this was as real was it was going to get.

"Don't worry," Jake said. "They don't go wild like real Horses. They're tamed now that they have Saddles on them."

Rosie nodded nervously and they began riding. She started out slow first on the pure white, nimbly trying to get hold of how she was supposed to maneuver. The Horse was slow and neighed obediently.

"Go faster, Rosie," Jake egged. "You ride like my grandma."

Rosie laughed and gave the Horse a small kick. It began treading faster…then faster…and then it began to galloped right past Jake and Olaf. Olaf whooped for joy and cupped a hand over his mouth.

"Ride like the wind, Rosie!" he yelled.

"Wait for me!" Jake cried.

Rosie stooped forward and let the white steed speed up. The wind was blowing nicely on her face, defeating the sun's hot rays on her skin. She passed dune after dune, looked as the hills in the distance became larger and larger in vision. They passed by another set of thick woods, but spread out enough for the Horses to pass by at their speed. She stroked the Horse as they reached a small hill. You can jump it, she said in her mind. No, we, can jump it. She let the Horse reach the tip before it lifted up into the air and over the small hill. Rosie let out a scream of surprise and delight.

Olaf and Jake eventually caught up with her and they road onwards until they hit the sea bank at the edge of the woods. Rosie looked at the coordinates screen, but didn't need to in order to understand that the island in the middle of the water was where they were heading to.

"It's just there," Rosie said. "It really is just there."

"Yeah," Olaf said. "Let's leave the Horses free and go on Boats."

Rosie nodded. She stroked her white Horse one more time and whispered a small Thank you. The Horse whinnied before heading off into the woods with the other Horses. If I had a name tag, I would have named it, Rosie said. But that wasn't what was important at the moment. She crafted an axe and cut down enough Oak Wood for three Boats and handed one each to Olaf and

Jake. They got on the Boats and drifted towards the island: a tiny mound of Grass and Dirt blocks with a Stone Brick stairway leading down. It was only then that it occurred to Rosie a question she should've asked herself the first minute the portal had been mentioned. What kind of portal is it? Rosie said. I highly doubt it's a Nether Portal. The only other portal I know of is the End Port—

The image of her dream returned to her. The floating island of End Stone, the tall Obsidian towers, Endermen staring at the sky and the flapping of wings...the husky, low voice that made her want to scream, the one she only recalled from her dream now.

"Rosie?" Olaf called.

Rosie started and shook her head. Olaf was already on land with Jake.

"Rosie?" Olaf repeated. "You're Boat's not moving. You look like you kind of spaced out."

Rosie started at the two for awhile, still shaken by the brief image she had seen. She managed to give them a wan smile.

"S-sorry," she said. "I guess I just can't believe it's our last day here."

Olaf and Jake smiled at her as she reached land.

"Yeah," Jake said. "The last day here…"

Loading Terrain…

Chapter 8: Final Boss

Rosie's heart was pounding as they descended down the stairs. She didn't know why, really, but it felt more like the premonition of something bad rather than good.

"Yikes," Jake suddenly said.

Rosie looked to where he was pointing. Bunch of items were floating on the floor with one Silverfish crawling on the floor. It wasn't like the silverfish you saw in old books. Minecraft Silverfish were at least the size of a foot and they were fat, crawling up and down, pouncing on players. Olaf sliced it down while picking up the things. Rosie found herself holding Nether Wart.

"I think it's what I picked up," Rosie said. "Do you think Luke died?"

Olaf shrugged.

"Either that or he dropped all this stuff here," he answered. He then picked up a Diamond Sword. "Then again, maybe not…"

Rosie was worried on both ends. It was possible that Luke might have died, but it was also possible that he was waiting on the other side, waiting to PK them. She then plucked up the courage to look at what she didn't want to see. There was a small set of stairs leading to pale stones with wide, animal eyes embedded in each. A void of black and particles floated in the middle. Rosie knew the pale blocks were End Portal blocks and that the eyes were Eyes of Ender. She also knew that jumping into the void would bring them to the supposed final destination of all players of Minecraft…

"This is the coordinates, alright," Jake said. "x: 616 z: 358…"

Rosie felt like biting her lips.

"It's the only portal here," Olaf said. "I say we go in."

"Me too," Jake agreed. "Rosie?"

Her name made her shiver a bit, but as she looked to her new friends she felt slightly eased.

"I'm scared," Rosie said. "But I know I'm not going anywhere without you guys."

She felt herself smile and the two boys smiled, too. Without having to say anything more to one another, they held hands and slowly climbed up the small stairs. The void seemed to stare at them like a giant, empty black pupil.

"On three?" Olaf asked. Rosie and Jake nodded.

"One…two…three…"

The End?

***

It was the sound again and that drove her insane. Static and whispery screeches filled her ears like tangible things, drilling into her eardrums like little earwigs as she slept. It was dark, but at the same time she could see. And then she felt the floor beneath her feet, her lungs breathing air and a cold chill running all over her body. She looked in front of her to see empty space save for the Obsidian towers and floor of End Stone. But the moment she looked around, her heart seemed to stop. She was alone. She walked a bit, warily scanning the area for Endermen, but more importantly, her teammates.

"Olaf?" she called. "Jake?"

"Rosie!" a shout from a beyond called. "Rosie, we're over here!"

Rosie's heart began beating again and relief washed over her. She ran as fast as she could, tired, drained, but driven to see her two friends in this world she hated so much.

"Olaf! Jake!" she yelled again.

She could now see them. Olaf's hideous username madpatata83 hovering over his head and Jake in his Creeper skin (Had anyone ever been so glad to see a Creeper!?). They began running towards her, too, waving.

"Rosie!" they called in unison.

"Guys!" she cried out, almost tearing in happiness.

A small fwoop! rushed through the air followed by a tick!

"Gah!" Olaf yelled. He recoiled to the side, pushing Jake with him. An arrow was sticking out of Olaf's head. Rosie stopped running and turned to where it had come from, anger and terror filling her at the same time as she screamed.

"Luke!" she yelled.

In the far distance, Luke was standing near the Obsidian, bow and arrow in hand, dressed completely in Diamond Armor.

"Hello, losers," he said. "Did you miss me?"

Rosie couldn't speak, but Olaf screamed as he charged towards Luke with a Diamond Sword.

"Olaf, don't!" Jake cried.

Luke lifted up his bow again and stretched it. Olaf ran in a zigzag, similar to how he had when he dodged the Wither's skulls.

"You monster!" Olaf cried as he lifted his sword into the air.

Luke didn't shoot and switched to a Diamond Sword as well. The two blades connected and clashed against each other. Olaf growled as he tried to force his blade down on Luke.

"You seem pretty upset," Luke smirked. "You that upset about me attacking you earlier."

Luke's blade pressed harder on Olaf's, the tip of the blade only inches from his head.

"No," Olaf said in a low voice. "But you killed those two other players…or maybe you killed more!?"

Olaf's blade left Luke's and swung to the side. Luke rolled over and kicked Olaf's feet, sending him down. Luke jumped on top but Olaf's blade prevented him from hitting.

"Olaf!" Rosie cried.

"Don't get close!" Olaf shouted. "Try to find the exit! Find it!"

Luke seemed to laugh at that.

"You're trying to play the hero, aren't you!?" Luke guffawed. "That's just sick, man! That's abnormal! You're supposed to look out for yourself!"

Olaf roared and pulled forward, kneeling to the ground and swinging his blade again, clashing each time as he hit that of Luke's but not getting a single scratch on him.

"You're abnormal!" Olaf said. "You're the bogey, aren't you!? You're working for REDNE!"

Luke pushed Olaf back and laughed again, this time high and almost maniacal.

"Working for REDNE!?" Luke said. "I am REDNE!"

The laugh became louder and louder and deep and distorted. Luke lifted into the air, his image blinking and changing. First it was his skin avatar flickering. And then it was the Steve-skinned avatar they had seen in Limbo. It kept flickering and changing until it turned into a black cloak with glaring red eyes.

"Idiots!" REDNE cried. "Did you really think there was a good end for you in store? Did you really think I'd reward you!? This is my world! And you are my players!"

Rosie and Jake approached Olaf and stood by him at the sides.

"You have no right to keep us here, REDNE!" Olaf shouted. "Let us and everyone else go!"

REDNE laughed again.

"Or what?" REDNE asked.

"Or we'll defeat you," Olaf said.

REDNE shook his head, he glared straight into Olaf's black pupils, hovering from above like a god looking down on a mortal.

"Such bravado," REDNE said. "Can you really defeat me? Fine. I'll give you a chance to fight and we'll see just how much of a hero you'll be then."

"You won't win!" Rosie's voice came.

It was so surprising that it took REDNE off guard for a bit—almost as much as it did for Rosie herself. But she didn't back down. She stepped forward.

"You won't win," Rosie said again. "Olaf's not alone. We're fighting with him."

"Yeah," Jake said. "We've made it this far together and we're going to make it through again."

REDNE floated there for awhile, silent. And then he looked at each of them, his words sending a chill up each of their spines.

"So be it."

REDNE drew his cape and flew high into the air. The sound of static arrived and suddenly Endermen were all around. They stood at the sides, flickering and fazing like bad cable TV, staring at the three. Everyone drew their swords.

They opened their mouths like gaping holes and then stared upwards.

Rooooooaaaaaaar….

Heavy flapping sounds came from above and the three players looked up. A large black dragon soared high above them, its wings so wide it case a shadow over the center of the floating island. Its purple eyes stared at them.

"ENDER…" Rosie whispered. "His name's not REDNE, it's ENDER. He's the Ender Dragon!"

The large Ender Dragon roared again, its yowl accompanied by the screeches of the Endermen.

"FIGHT ME THEN!" the distorted voice of ENDER came and he swooped down.

"DODGE!" Olaf cried.

The three jumped in different directions as ENDER touched the floor and soared high up again. The Endermen left the sides of the End Stone walls and began walking, closing in on the players.

"Keep to the walls Obsidian!" Olaf yelled again.

Rosie ran to the closest wall and kept her back to it. An Enderman charged towards her. She remembered something. Stare at them and they won't teleport. Her heart was beating wildly but she lifted her face and yelled out her fears while chopping at the Enderman who couldn't leave now that she was glaring at it. It fell with a wounded cry and dropped an Ender Pearl.

"We need to get to break the Ender Crystals on top!" Jake suddenly cried from a distance. "Use the pearls!"

Rosie understood at once and followed after them as they each climbed by putting block by block under their feet. When she got close enough she threw the Ender Pearl. Rosie flashed from her position and to the top of the Obsidian tower. The Orb floated before her, sending a ray to ENDER. The Ender Crystals heal him, she remembered again from her old game files. She stood a small distance from it and hit it with her sword. It exploded on impact and ENDER gave out a cry.

"Rosie!" Olaf said. "Look out!"

Rosie turned around as the ENDER charged down towards her. She jumped and hung onto the ledge, she could see his belly. She almost dropped, but she held on for dear life and pulled herself up. Olaf continued shooting the other Ender Crystals from his tower and Jake was doing the same. Rosie leapt down to cling onto her small Cobblestone pile and then got on it. She dug down and built near another tower. Olaf was shooting and three more Ender Crystals went down, bam, bam, bam!

Rosie took out another two and Jake another. ENDER cried out in rage.

"There's one more!" Olaf said.

Rosie looked around and saw it. She climbed up again and got to it. She took her sword and sliced at it.

Roooooooooooooooooooaaaaarrrr!!!!!

ENDER yowled in anger and charged at Rosie from behind. Rosie didn't have the time to think and the tail of the dragon flicked her off the tower.

"Rosie!" Olaf yelled.

Rosie screamed as she headed down, but stopped. She was going to die. She knew that know. If she was going to die, she didn't want it to be out of fright. She closed her eyes, tears falling from her cheeks. I'm sorry, guys…she said to herself. You'll have to do this without me.

Water splashed from below her and Rosie was bobbing in water again. Jake stood before her, his Creeper face smiling.

"Jake!" Rosie screamed in happiness as she embraced him.

"Glad to see you, too," Jake said.

ENDER screeched again as Olaf shot arrow after arrow at him. Rosie noticed something else that wasn't in Olaf's bow earlier. It was glowing. Olaf's bow glowed a faint shimmering purple now and as ENDER drew closer to him, it shone even brighter.

"I am your END!" ENDER cried. "END NOW!"

But Olaf only shook his head.

"No, Ender," Olaf said. "This is only the end for you."

The bow shone a bright white just as ENDER closed in. Olaf let go of the bow and a bright white light flashed before everyone.

"NOOOOOOOOOOOOOOO!" ENDER cried. "I don't understand! This is my world! MINE!"

No, it's not...it's never been...

"I'll come back! I swear on it, Mojang! I'll come back and rule it all over again!!!!"

You're forgetting your place, Ender. You don't own The World. The players do. You're just another mob for them to defeat.

"AAAAAAAAAAAAAAAAAAaaaaaaaaaaarGGGG H!!!!!!"

When Rosie could look again, she, Jake and Olaf were all standing next to one another. The Endermen were gone and the entire biome was silent. In front of them stood the End Portal and an Egg on top.

"Is it over?" Jake asked.

"I don't know," Olaf said. "I don't know how it ended like that, either."

Rosie looked at the Egg. Unlike in the Minecraft game, though, this egg wasn't black and purple but rather orange with red spots. Rosie reached out for it and touched it. It glowed white and floated before them.

Thank you for saving The World… a soft, distorted, but pleasant voice said. You've conquered the Ender Dragon and have ended his cruel rule.

The three players stood there silently, unable to speak.

Everyone's safe now…the voice said. Even those who died in game. All of you will be teleported home once you three step into this portal.

"Is it really over?" Rosie asked.

The worst is over, yes. But not the game…you will play as you will. This game is endless, after all.

Rosie looked to the Egg (was it even that, still?) and then lowered her head.

"Thank you for helping us," she said. "We know you were the one who empowered Olaf's bow."

It was your will, the voice said. I only put its power into the weapon, but it was the power of all you, just the same.

"Thank you," Olaf then said.

"Yeah, thanks," Jake followed.

Thanking time is over…the voice said. Off with you and be on your way home.

The three listened and stepped into the portal, letting the darkness envelop them, but no longer being afraid.

The End.

Chapter 9: New Game

It was the strangest thing Rosie had ever been, through, yes and everyone had woken up in the convention room. Rosie eventually got to meet Jake and Olaf in person. She was now waking from a small nap in her own room. She wasn't in her bed, but the PC was on and the Minecraft was running. She had placed it on pause. She resumed the game and saw she was playing one of her old game files. It was a nice Snow biome and she was building a small Spruce Wood house. Her cell phone buzzed. There were two messages.

Mad Potato Olaf:

Hey, you going online or what? Let us know.

Redstone Eng. Jake:

Rooooosiiieeee…we have a date. Or is triple date since Olaf is here (I can get really jealous, though).

Rosie smiled and replied to each of them. She then exited her game and opened the Multiplayer tab. There were no servers there except for one server.

It's a permanent server. It will always be there for you who have visited. It's your reward, privilege and right.

The server's name was a simple one, but powerful all the same: The World.

Rosie clicked it.

It's a game you can play whenever you want and one that has changed your life forever.

Rosie selected The World and white letters came before her on a Dirt pixel background.

Click OK to change your reality…

A small smile came to Rosie's lips and she didn't hesitate clicking for a second.

CPSIA information can be obtained at www.ICGtesting.com
Printed in the USA
LVOW05s1303181114

414313LV00001B/63/P